MR MAJEIKA AND THE LOST SPELL BOOK

Humphrey Carpenter (1946–2005), the author and creator of *Mr Majeika*, was born and educated in Oxford. He went to a school called the Dragon School where exciting things often happened and there were some very odd teachers – you could even call it magical! He became a full-time writer in 1975 and was the author of many award-winning biographies. As well as the *Mr Majeika* titles, his children's books also included *Shakespeare Without the Boring Bits* and *More Shakespeare Without the Boring Bits*. He wrote plays for radio and theatre and founded the children's drama group The Mushy Pea Theatre Company. He played the tuba, double bass, bass saxophone and keyboard.

Humphrey once said, "The nice thing about being a writer is that you can make magic happen without learning tricks. Words are the only tricks you need. I can write: 'He floated up to the ceiling, and a baby rabbit came out of his pocket, grew wings, and flew away.' And you will believe that it really happened! That's magic, isn't it?"

HUMPHREY CARPENTER

Mr Majeika and the
Lost Spell Book

Illustrated by Frank Rodgers

PUFFIN

PUFFIN BOOKS

Published by the Penguin Group
Penguin Books Ltd, 80 Strand, London WC2R 0RL, England
Penguin Putnam Inc., 375 Hudson Street, New York, New York 10014, USA
Penguin Books Australia Ltd, 250 Camberwell Road, Camberwell,
Victoria 3124, Australia
Penguin Books Canada Ltd, 10 Alcorn Avenue, Toronto, Ontario, Canada M4V 3B2
Penguin Books India (P) Ltd, 11 Community Centre, Panchsheel Park,
New Delhi – 110 017, India
Penguin Books (NZ) Ltd, Cnr Rosedale and Airborne Roads, Albany, Auckland,
New Zealand
Penguin Books (South Africa) (Pty) Ltd, 24 Sturdee Avenue, Rosebank 2196, South Africa

Penguin Books Ltd, Registered Offices: 80 Strand, London WC2R 0RL, England

www.penguin.com

First published 2003
001

Text copyright © Humphrey Carpenter, 2003
Illustrations copyright © Frank Rodgers, 2003
All rights reserved

The moral right of the author and illustrator has been asserted

Set in Palatino

Made and printed in England by Clays Ltd, St Ives plc

British Library Cataloguing in Publication Data
A CIP catalogue record for this book is available from the British Library

ISBN-13: 978–0–141–34696–0

www.greenpenguin.co.uk

ALWAYS LEARNING   **PEARSON**

Contents

Contents

1. Mr Potter's Rules

'Now, children,' said Mr Potter, the head teacher of St Barty's School, at morning Assembly, 'tonight – as I'm sure all of you know – is Halloween.'

Everyone felt very excited when he said that, because Halloween was one of the most special days of the year. Maybe even more exciting than Christmas, because you could dress up as witches and wizards, and have lots of fun.

'This year,' Mr Potter went on, 'I am going to make some rules for Halloween.'

Jody and the twins, Thomas and Pete, who were all in Class Three together, looked gloomily at each other. Halloween wasn't the sort of time that you wanted rules. It was all about having fun.

'We need to protect the good name of the school,' said Mr Potter. 'I don't want people to say that children from St Barty's behave badly on Halloween. So here are the rules. You mustn't frighten old ladies. You mustn't wear masks that cover your whole face, because it's very frightening for old ladies – and old men – to open the front door and see people in terrifying disguises. You must only wear little masks that cover your eyes. Don't say "trick or treat" when people open the door, because I don't want you to play tricks on anyone, even if they don't give you sweets. And if they do give you treats, you must say thank you very politely. Please remember these rules. I shall get very cross if people don't keep them. Now you can go to your classrooms.'

'That spoils everything,' said Thomas to Pete and Jody, as they were walking across the playground to Class Three.

'Oh, I don't know,' said Jody. 'We can still have a lot of fun, even if we keep Mr Potter's rules.'

'I'm sure Hamish Bigmore wouldn't agree with you, Jody,' said Thomas. 'And where is he? I didn't see him in Assembly this morning. It's not like him to be late for school, even though he is the worst-behaved boy in Class Three.'

'I reckon we should forget all about Halloween,' said Pete gloomily. 'Something always goes wrong during it. Do you remember the year that all three of us dressed up as ghosts?'

'Oh, that was fun,' said Jody. 'Your mum made us lovely ghost costumes out of old sheets, with holes cut for our eyes.'

'Yes,' said Thomas, 'but we couldn't see out of them properly, and don't you remember what happened?'

'We went to Mr Potter's house,' said Pete, 'and when we tried to find our way up the path to his front door, we got completely lost and fell into his pond.'

'We were covered in slime,' said Thomas. 'Yuck!'

'I've got an idea,' said Jody. 'We could keep Mr Potter's rules, and still have an exciting time. Guess what my idea is!'

'Is it something to do with Mr Majeika?' asked Pete. Mr Majeika was Class Three's teacher. Before he came to St Barty's, he had been a wizard, and he still did magic spells sometimes, though he wasn't supposed to.

'Yes, it is,' said Jody. 'Look, here he comes now. Mr Majeika, could you help us with Halloween?'

'What's Halloween?' asked Mr Majeika. He still didn't know lots of things about ordinary life on earth, because he'd been a wizard somewhere up in the sky, or wherever it was that wizards came from, for a very long time, and he'd only been a teacher for a little while.

'Halloween happens once a year,' said Thomas, 'and it's very exciting, because we all dress up as witches and wizards and ghosts and other scary things like that, and knock on people's doors.'

'And when they open them,' said Pete, 'we say, "Trick or treat?"'

'And if they say "Treat",' said Jody, 'it means they're going to give us sweets, or bars of chocolate, or some other nice thing.'

'But if they say "Trick", it means they'd rather we play a trick on them, like dangling a rubber spider in their face,' Thomas explained.

'That's interesting,' said Mr Majeika. 'In the land of the wizards, we have a night like that. It's called Ordinary People Night, and we all dress up as ordinary people. We stop wearing our wizard and witch hats and cloaks, and put on trousers and shirts and dresses and things – the sort of clothes that you wear down here on earth. And we stop doing spells and magic, and do things like going to school, or to ordinary jobs.'

'It doesn't sound very exciting, Mr Majeika,' said Pete.

'Oh, but it is,' said Mr Majeika. 'It's a great change from spending our days and nights doing magic.'

'We wanted to ask you to help us, Mr Majeika,' said Jody. 'You see, Mr Potter won't let us wear exciting costumes and masks for Halloween tonight. So I was wondering if you could help us by doing a bit of magic.'

'What sort of magic?' asked Mr Majeika. 'You know I'm not supposed to do any at all. That was what the Chief Wizard told me when he sent me down to earth to be a teacher. "Remember, Majeika," he said to me, "not the slightest bit of magic! You mustn't even open your spell book, or wave your magic wand, otherwise there will be dreadful trouble."'

'Yes, but you *have* done magic, quite often, Mr Majeika, since you became a teacher,' said Thomas.

'Almost as soon as you arrived at St Barty's,' said Pete, 'you started doing magic. Surely you remember the time when you turned Hamish Bigmore into a frog?'

'And there have been lots of times since then,' said Jody. 'I don't think that more than a week has gone by without you doing some sort of magic in Class Three.'

Mr Majeika gave a shudder. 'Please don't remind me!' he said. 'If the Chief Wizard knew only half of all the magic

I've done since I came here, I would be in dreadful trouble.'

'What sort of trouble?' asked Thomas. But before Mr Majeika had time to answer, there was a horrible cackling noise from the passage outside Class Three.

'Fee, fi, fo, fum,' chanted a voice, 'I will bite you on the bum! I'll sink my teeth into anyone weaker, especially the neck of Mr Majeika!' The door opened, and in burst Count Dracula.

At least, for a moment they thought it really was Dracula. Then they realized it was just Hamish Bigmore, in a very expensive Dracula costume.

'Are you going to wear that for Halloween tonight, Hamish?' said Jody. 'Because I don't think Mr Potter will like it at all. He told us that we mustn't wear anything that might frighten people.'

'Silly old Piggy-face Potter,' said Hamish. 'Who cares what he thinks?'

'Now, Hamish,' said Mr Majeika, 'you're not to speak of Mr Potter like that.'

'Mr Majeika is being very kind,' said Pete. 'He's agreed to use a little magic to give us a more exciting Halloween.'

'He hasn't agreed to do it yet,' said Jody.

'But I'm sure he will if we ask him really nicely.'

'Well,' said Mr Majeika, 'I'm sure a *little* magic can't do any harm, especially on an evening when everyone is dressed up as witches and wizards and ghosts.'

'Oh, thank you, Mr Majeika,' said Thomas. 'It will make all the difference to our Halloween.'

'Yes, thank you, Mr Majeika,' said Hamish Bigmore, with a nasty smile. 'Thank you very much.' And he went out of the classroom to take off his Dracula costume in the boys' changing room.

'That's very odd,' said Jody. 'I've never heard Hamish saying thank you before, especially to Mr Majeika. I'm sure he's up to something.'

2. Cousin Lulubelle

At half past six that evening, they all met outside the school gates, wearing their Halloween costumes. Jodie had come as a green-faced witch; her hat and cloak were green as well. 'My mum made my costume,' she said to Thomas and Pete, 'and she found some green make-up for my face. It looks good, doesn't it?'

'Oh yes, very good,' said Pete, though actually he thought it was rather a dull costume. He and Thomas had come all in black, with pointed wizards' hats that had silver stars and moons stuck on them.

'I like your hats,' said Jody, though actually she thought that they looked dull too.

Everyone else had done their best with their costumes, but nobody's was really exciting. One or two people had dressed up as skeletons or ghosts, but it all looked rather feeble. 'I wonder what Hamish will do,' said Thomas. 'Do you think he will pay no attention to what Mr Potter said, and come in his Dracula costume?'

Just at that moment, a big shiny car drew up at the school gates. The driver was a woman, and in the front passenger seat sat Hamish Bigmore. He wound down the window and called out, 'Hi there, everyone!'

'What's he doing in that car?' wondered Pete. 'It's not his mum and dad's.'

Hamish climbed out of the car. They

could see he wasn't wearing any sort of Halloween costume – he was just in his ordinary school clothes.

'I want you all to meet my American cousin,' he said to them. 'Her name is Lulubelle Bigmore.'

Lulubelle got out of the car. She was a peculiar shape for a woman, and she had lots and lots of very bright yellow hair. From a strap round her neck hung a very large camera, with an enormous lens.

'Why, hi there, all you little kiddiewinks,' she said in a drawling American accent. 'I hope you don't mind little Hamish's Cousin Lulubelle coming to join in the fun.'

'Er, no,' said Thomas, a bit uncertainly.

'Of course, we have Halloween back home, in old Virginia, where I come from,' said Lulubelle, 'but I reckon all you little British kiddiewinks do things a little differently.'

Just then, Mr Majeika arrived. He had a strange-looking stick with him. It was all sparkly and covered with stars. 'Is that your magic wand, Mr Majeika?' asked Jody. 'We've never seen you use one before.'

Mr Majeika nodded. 'That's right, Jody,' he said. 'I very rarely take it out of its drawer – I don't normally need it to do a spell. But I think tonight is going to be a special night, so I brought it along with me. Now,' he continued, looking around at Class Three and their rather bedraggled costumes, 'let's see what we can do. Everyone must shut their eyes while I find the right spell for the job.'

They all closed their eyes – all except Hamish Bigmore and Cousin Lulubelle. Mr Majeika took a deep breath and then said a lot of very strange words while he waved his left hand in the air, and (with his right hand) pointed his wand at each of them, one by one. For a moment, they all felt a bit peculiar, as if they were being turned upside down and shaken. Then everything seemed normal again, and they opened their eyes.

What they saw was, at first, so frightening that they nearly screamed. Each of Class Three found themselves surrounded by real-life witches, wizards, skeletons and ghosts. It was only when everyone realized that they themselves were a witch, a wizard, a ghost or a skeleton as well that they stopped being frightened, and started to laugh and even cheer.

'Hooray!' shouted Thomas, who had turned into a very funny-looking wizard with a long nose and a big droopy moustache. 'This is the best spell you've ever done, Mr Majeika.'

'I agree,' said Pete, who was a very tall, very thin wizard with knobbly knees, and a beard that came down to his feet.

'Well done, Mr Majeika!' said Jody, who was a short, fat witch – not as nasty to look at as Wilhelmina Worlock, the witch who was always causing trouble for Class Three, but still quite frightening. 'What shall we all do now?'

'Hey, folks,' called out Lulubelle Bigmore, 'you all look great, so smile at the camera, everyone!' And she began to take lots and lots of photos of them.

'Now, everyone,' called out Mr Majeika, 'there's no time to waste – the spell will wear off in an hour from now. So off you go, as quickly as you can.'

'Where should we go, Mr Majeika?' asked Jody.

'Oh, silly me,' said Mr Majeika. 'I quite forgot to give you your broomsticks.'

Once again he waved his hand and his wand in the air – and suddenly they all had broomsticks. 'Up into the sky with you,' he said. 'See who can fly the fastest!'

The next hour was the most exciting time that Thomas, Pete, Jody and the rest of Class Three had ever known in their lives. At first they just zoomed around in the sky, learning how to ride on their broomsticks. Then, as they got more confident, they began to fly down to people's houses, where they knocked on the doors and surprised all the people living there, before they zoomed up into the sky again. 'We mustn't go near Mr Potter's house,' warned Jody, and they took care to keep away from it.

Meanwhile, on the ground, Lulubelle was driving her car – with Hamish in the passenger seat – and stopping to take photographs whenever she saw a witch, a wizard, a skeleton or a ghost. She also took lots of pictures of Mr Majeika.

At last, Mr Majeika looked at his watch and called out, 'Time's up!'

One by one, they flew back on their broomsticks to the school gates – though Thomas and Pete couldn't resist having a sky-battle on their way back. Each of them tried to knock the other off his broomstick, until Mr Majeika called to them to stop and behave themselves.

As soon as everyone was back, Mr Majeika lined them up, so that he could do a spell that would change them back into their ordinary selves.

'Hang on there a minute, kiddiewinks,' said Lulubelle Bigmore. 'I want just one more lovely picture of you all and your clever, magical teacher.'

'Do you think we could have copies of the photographs, please?' asked Thomas.

'You bet you can,' said Hamish, with a nasty grin. 'In fact, anyone can get copies of these pictures tomorrow morning just by going down to their newspaper shop. This isn't really my cousin.' And he pulled off Lulubelle's blonde wig, so that they could see that 'Lulubelle' was really a man.

'Allow me to introduce myself,' he said, holding out his hand to Mr Majeika. 'I'm

Dennis Prott of the *Moon* newspaper –
and tomorrow morning you'll all be on
the front page.'

'Yes, Mr Majeika,' said Hamish
Bigmore, very nastily. 'You're in real
trouble now!'

3. The Governors Decide

Thomas and Pete found it very difficult to sleep that night. Early the next morning, they went down the road to the newspaper shop. Sure enough, the headline on the front page of the *Moon* was: 'WOULD YOU WANT YOUR KIDS TAUGHT BY THIS MAN?' The picture showed Mr Majeika waving his magic wand. Beneath it were these words:

'Ace reporter of the *Moon*, Dennis Prott, has discovered WITCHCRAFT being

taught to LITTLE CHILDREN in one of
Britain's most innocent-looking
SCHOOLS. He watched while evil sorcerer
Mr Majeika waved his MAGIC WAND
and chanted FOUL SPELLS over the
CHILDREN, turning them into VICIOUS-
LOOKING WITCHES AND WIZARDS.
He listened while Mr Majeika taught his
VICTIMS to play NASTY TRICKS on OLD
LADIES. He gasped in amazement while
this WICKED WIZARD passed on to the
children the SECRETS of his BLACK ART.

'The *Moon* asks, HOW LONG CAN
THIS BE ALLOWED TO GO ON? The
Moon says, NOT A DAY, NOT AN HOUR
LONGER. The *Moon* demands, SACK MR
MAJEIKA NOW!!!'

'Oh dear,' sighed Thomas, 'it's even
worse than we expected. What do you
think we should do?'

They went home and phoned Jody. She had already seen the *Moon*. 'Do you think we should phone Mr Majeika and warn him, before he gets to school?' she asked.

'That's a good idea,' said Pete. 'But does anyone know his home telephone number?'

'I wouldn't bet that he's even got a telephone,' said Jody. 'He doesn't seem the sort of person who would.'

'Maybe we could get in touch with him by telepathy,' said Thomas.

'By what?' asked Pete.

'Telepathy,' said Thomas. 'It's when somebody thinks something, and they manage to make somebody else know what they're thinking.'

'Oh, don't be stupid,' said Jody on the phone. 'You're just wasting time – it can't possibly work.'

'You never know,' said Thomas. 'It

won't take a moment to try it. Let's practise before we try to contact Mr Majeika. I'll think hard,' he said to Pete, 'and you've got to tell me what I'm thinking about.'

Thomas thought hard. He thought about a car – a big, red, shiny sports car. In his imagination, he thought about himself driving it very fast, at a hundred miles an hour. The car had its roof folded down, so that the wind was roaring through Thomas's hair. He was having a wonderful time.

'What was I thinking about?' he asked Pete.

'You were thinking about eating a banana,' said Pete.

Thomas was very disappointed. 'It didn't work,' he told Jody down the telephone.

'We *must* stop wasting time,' Jody said.

'Let's get to school as quickly as possible, so that we can try to keep Mr Majeika out of trouble.'

They hurried off to school. As soon as they got there, they saw a big crowd of men and women around the gates. All were holding cameras, microphones or notebooks. And in the middle of them were Dennis Prott and Hamish Bigmore.

'Hi there, kiddiewinks,' said Dennis in

his Lulubelle voice. 'Look at all the friends I've brought with me today. They're all waiting to talk to your naughty teacher – he's going to be on lots of radio and TV programmes, and in all the other newspapers.'

'That's nice,' said Thomas.

'No, it isn't,' said Jody. 'He's going to get into awful trouble – it's the worst thing that Hamish Bigmore has ever done to him.'

Hamish grinned nastily at Jody, and waved Dennis's 'Lulubelle' wig in the air. Pete grabbed it from him, and tried to tear it in half. Then he changed his mind, and ran off with it, calling to Thomas and Jody to follow him.

'Listen,' he said, when they had caught up with him, 'I've got an idea. If we can find Mr Majeika and stop him before –'

'Here I am,' said Mr Majeika. He was

walking past them on his way to school. 'What a lovely sunny morning it is,' he said cheerfully.

'It may be sunny,' said Jody, 'but it's not lovely at all, Mr Majeika, at least not for us.' And she explained to him what had happened.

Five minutes later, they put Pete's idea into action.

Pete pushed through the crowd of reporters and TV and radio people and shouted rude things at Hamish Bigmore, until Hamish lost his temper and tried to hit Pete, who ran away. Hamish ran after him. This was what Pete had wanted – it was important to get Hamish out of the way before his plan could be carried out.

Then Thomas and Jody walked up to the crowd at the school gates, with a third person walking between them.

'Let us through, please,' said Jody. 'This

is our dinner lady, Mrs Maggs, and she's not feeling very well this morning.'

The reporters and TV and radio people let them through, but Dennis Prott had a suspicious look on his face, so they hurried across the playground as quickly as possible, and in through the main door of the school. Too quickly, because Mr Potter was just inside the door and he bumped straight into 'Mrs Maggs', whose

hair fell off – because she was, of course, Mr Majeika, disguised in Dennis Prott's Lulubelle wig. Fortunately, the reporters couldn't see what was happening indoors.

'Ah, Majeika,' said Mr Potter, 'I was just looking for you. The governors of the school are holding a special meeting and they want you to come to it.'

'Can we come too, Mr Potter?' asked Jody.

Mr Potter shook his head and led Mr Majeika off by the arm.

'It's all right,' said Pete. 'They're meeting in Mr Potter's office, which is next door to Class Three, and if you go into the big cupboard in the classroom, there's a hole in the wall, and you can see and hear what's being said in the office.'

They hurried into the classroom. There was only room for one person in the cupboard, so Jody went into it and told the others what she could see and hear through the hole.

'There are just two governors,' she said in a whisper. 'One of them is a very old man with a long beard, who seems to be asleep, and the other is – oh no! – it's Hamish Bigmore's mum!'

'What's she doing in there?' said Thomas.

'She became a school governor last term,' said Pete.

'Shh!' said Jody. 'Mr Potter is introducing Mr Majeika to the old man, who's fallen fast asleep again already. And now Mr Potter is reading out bits from the *Moon* about Mr Majeika doing magic, and Mr Majeika is looking very unhappy. Mrs Bigmore is getting very angry and saying that Mr Potter ought to sack Mr Majeika right away. And now –

oh, bother – Mr Potter has taken off his
jacket, and hung it on a hook just above
the hole in the wall, and I can't see or hear
anything any more. We'll just have to wait
until Mr Majeika comes out.

They had to wait for a long while, and
when Mr Majeika finally came into Class

Three, he looked very miserable.

'Have you been given the sack, Mr Majeika?' asked Thomas.

Mr Majeika shook his head. 'Not quite,' he answered. 'Mrs Bigmore wanted Mr Potter to fire me at once, but instead he's told me that I can go on teaching if I promise to give up all magic. So I've promised that I'll break my magic wand, and burn my spell book.'

'That's terrible, Mr Majeika,' said Jody. 'Worse than the sack.'

Mr Majeika nodded. 'It means I can never be a wizard again, for the rest of my life. And I've promised to do it right away.' He took his wand out of the drawer, shut his eyes and bent the wand double, so that Jody, Thomas and Pete were certain it would break. But instead, it vanished!

'Oh dear,' said Mr Majeika, 'I must have

said a vanishing spell over it by accident.'

'Well, you *tried* to break it, Mr Majeika,' said Jody.

'I suppose so,' said Mr Majeika anxiously. 'But I'll have to make sure my spell book really does catch on fire. Here it is,' he said, pulling it out from its hiding place under his desk. 'Has anyone got a box of matches?'

Nobody had. 'Surely, Mr Majeika,' said Jody, 'you could do a fire spell to make it burn?'

Mr Majeika nodded. 'That's a good idea,' he said. He shut his eyes and waved his hands over the book.

Just at that moment, Hamish Bigmore barged noisily into the classroom. 'Yah, boo, sucks!' he shouted at Mr Majeika. 'You'll never be able to turn me into anything again, now that you've had to give up doing magic. Serves you right, silly old Mr Majeika.' Then suddenly Hamish yelled 'Ouch!' because the spell book had risen up in the air, and come down on top of him with a big thump.

'Oh dear,' said Mr Majeika, 'I didn't mean to do that at all – I must have used the wrong spell again.'

The book went on thumping Hamish, and when he tried to run away, it chased him round the classroom. At this moment, the door opened, and in came Mrs Bigmore, followed by Mr Potter.

'What is going on?' shrieked Mrs Bigmore.

'He's done another of his spells,' yelled Hamish, who was trying to hide from the spell book by squeezing under one of the desks. The book found him there quickly, and began to smack him on the bottom. 'Ow! Ow!' shrieked Hamish.

'That proves it!' said Mrs Bigmore. 'Mr Majeika obviously doesn't have the slightest intention of giving up magic. He's going to go on doing horrid magical things to my poor little Hamish. Sack him at once, Mr Potter! Sack him right now!'

Mr Potter nodded gloomily. 'I'm afraid

you're right,' he said to Mrs Bigmore.
'Mr Majeika, you must leave the school
at once, and never come back.'

4. What a Week

A week later, Thomas and Pete were walking home from school with Jody.

'What a dull week it's been,' said Pete. 'I knew that Mr Majeika's magic made school more exciting, but I never dreamed that school without magic could be so boring.'

'Well,' said Jody, 'we haven't been very lucky with teachers, have we?'

There had been a different teacher on each of the five days. On Monday, there had been an old man with a white moustache, who had shouted at them as if they were soldiers in the army under his command. But of course Hamish Bigmore had shouted back at him, so he told Mr Potter he wouldn't go on teaching Class Three.

On Tuesday, they were taught by a very fat man, who ate cream buns while they were writing or drawing. Hamish had stolen one of his buns and smeared it all over the drawings that were pinned on the wall, so of course he wouldn't come the next day either.

On Wednesday, there was a young woman with long hair. Hamish had tied her hair to the back of her chair, and by the time Jody and some of the other girls had managed to untie it, she had decided she wouldn't come back again either.

On Thursday, there had been a big tough man, who looked like a footballer

and arrived at school in an expensive-
looking car. He had managed to keep
Hamish under control, but when he left at
the end of school he found that Hamish
had poured glue into the door-locks of his
car, so he couldn't get into it.

And on Friday, no one would come to
teach Class Three, so Mr Potter had had

to do it himself, and very boring this had been.

'It was so dull with Mr Potter teaching us,' said Pete, 'that I reckon Hamish Bigmore must have been missing Mr Majeika too.'

'Look,' said Jody, 'there he is!'

'Do you mean Hamish?' asked Thomas.

'No – Mr Majeika!' Jody pointed across the street to the park. Mr Majeika was sitting on one of the benches. He was looking very miserable.

They ran over to him at once. 'What have you been doing all week, Mr Majeika?' Pete asked him.

'I've tried all sorts of different jobs,' he told them. 'I've been a postman, a milkman, a newspaper-delivery man, a gardener and a builder, but I always make silly mistakes and get the sack. When I was a postman, the letters I was carrying all blew away in the wind. When I was a milkman, I tripped over my own feet and dropped all the milk bottles, so that they broke. When I was delivering newspapers, there was a huge shower of rain, which turned all the papers into soggy sludge. When I was a gardener, I pulled up a root and the tree to which it belonged fell on top of me. And when I was a builder, all the scaffolding that I had put up fell down.'

'Poor Mr Majeika,' said Jody. 'You have had a lot of bad luck.'

'Oh, it wasn't luck,' said Mr Majeika. 'It was Wilhelmina Worlock.'

Wilhelmina Worlock was a wicked witch who had made a nuisance of herself to Mr Majeika ever since he had come to St Barty's School.

'You mean,' asked Pete, 'that she blew away the letters, tripped you, made it rain on the newspapers, pulled up the tree and pushed the scaffolding down?'

'Exactly,' said Mr Majeika. 'She was always invisible, but I knew it was her, because I could hear her cackling with laughter whenever things went wrong for me.'

'Couldn't you use magic to stop her, or to get your revenge?' asked Jody.

Mr Majeika shook his head sadly. 'I tried to, but it didn't work. I said the spells, but nothing happened. You see, my spell book vanished after it had finished chasing Hamish, and now when I shut my eyes and wave my hands, nothing magical happens at all.'

'Isn't there any way you can get your magic powers back again?' asked Pete.

Mr Majeika thought for a moment. 'Well,' he said, 'there is one way. But it would be impossible.'

'Tell us about it, Mr Majeika,' said Thomas.

'A long time ago,' said Mr Majeika, 'I was told by another wizard that, if I ever lost my magic powers while in this world, the thing to do would be to find the Old Back Door, which is a secret way into the place where all magic comes from. I asked him where the Old Back Door was, and he didn't know. But he did say that there was a map showing it. He said this map was the oldest in the world, and it was kept in the oldest library in the world. I asked him which was the oldest library in the world, and he told me that – good gracious, how *could* I have forgotten about that?' And suddenly, Mr Majeika was roaring with laughter.

'What is it, Mr Majeika?' asked Jody. 'What's so funny?'

'He told me,' explained Mr Majeika,

'that the oldest library in the world is in St Barty's Castle.'

'St Barty's Castle?' repeated Thomas in amazement. 'But that's just down the road!'

'Exactly,' said Mr Majeika. 'Come along – we can be there in five minutes!'

5. Who Stole the Map?

The castle was a big building near the railway station, made of old grey stone. Alongside a notice giving the opening hours and the ticket prices was a signpost that said: 'To the Oldest Library in the World'. They followed the direction in which the signpost was pointing, and found themselves at the back of the castle, where there was a very old-looking door with the word 'Library' painted on it. Above a big iron handle were the words 'Please Ring', so Thomas pulled the handle very hard, and they could hear the jangling of a bell some distance away.

For what seemed like a long time, nothing happened. Then suddenly a flap in the door sprang open, making them all jump, and a face poked through – the face of an old man with a beard.

'Y-y-y-y-yes?' he said very sharply, but with a stammer. 'You r-r-r-r-rang the b-b-b-b-bell?'

'We d-d-d-d-did,' said Thomas, who seemed to have caught the stammer from the old man. 'I mean,' he went on, without a stammer, 'we did. We want to see the map that shows the Old Back – ow!' He ended like this because Pete had just stepped on his toes, to shut him up. Pete thought it wasn't a good idea to mention the Old Back Door just yet.

'We'd like, please, to look at your collection of old maps,' Pete said.

'H-h-h-h-how old?' asked the old man, looking very suspiciously at Pete.

'Oh, very old indeed, please,' said Jody.

'And w-w-w-w-which of you wants to s-s-s-s-see them?' asked the old man, peering around at them all.

'Our teacher, Mr Majeika,' said Thomas, rubbing his foot where Pete had stood on it. 'He needs to see the map, so that he can discover the Old Back – *ow!*' Pete had stepped on his other foot.

'Mr Majeika?' repeated the old man. 'N-n-n-n-now where have I heard or seen that n-n-n-n-name before?' He looked Pete straight in the eye. 'Are *you* Mr Majeika?' he said.

Pete shook his head. 'No,' said the old man, 'I thought you weren't.'

He shifted his gaze to Thomas. 'Are *you* Mr Majeika? No? I thought not.' This time he looked at Jody. 'And *you* d-d-d-d-

definitely aren't Mr Majeika,' he said to
her, 'which leaves – *you*.'

Mr Majeika nodded.

'Yes, I thought so,' said the old man.
'Well,' he said to Mr Majeika, '*you* very d-
d-d-d-definitely *cannot* come into the
library.'

'What about us?' asked Jody.

'Ch-ch-ch-ch-children not allowed,'
snapped the old man, removing his face
and shutting the door-flap with a bang.

Thomas grabbed hold of the bell-handle, and was going to pull it again, but Pete said: 'No – it's no good arguing with someone like that. We need a better plan.' Then he whispered in Thomas and Jody's ears, and they both nodded, so Pete whispered the plan to Mr Majeika, who nodded as well. 'We'll have to go home first, to get the clothes,' said Pete. So off they all went to Thomas and Pete's house.

Half an hour later, a very strange-looking lady was walking along the path that led round the back of the castle, to the library. She was very tall, and bulged in some rather odd places, and she had lots of very bright yellow hair. She reached the library door, and rang the bell.

When the flap opened, and the old man peered out, the lady said, 'How do you do? I am Mrs Lulubelle Prott, and I would like to see your collection of old maps.'

'W-w-w-w-why, certainly, madam,' said the old man, opening the door. Mrs Prott stepped inside, and the old man shut the door behind her. 'D-d-d-d-do you have any particular map in mind?' he asked her.

'Well,' said Pete, because he was the top half of Mrs Prott, 'I'd like to see anything that shows *doors* – and very old ones, please.'

'C-c-c-come with me,' said the old man. He set off down a dark passage, and Mrs Prott tried to follow him, but her bottom half (who was Thomas) couldn't see where he was going, and bumped into the wall, so that Pete nearly fell off his shoulders.

'N-n-n-n-now,' said the old man, stopping by a door which said 'Map

Room', 'it sounds to me as if you need the map that shows the Old Back Door.'

Ten minutes later, Mrs Prott came out of the main door of the library into the open air. Waiting at the front of the castle were Mr Majeika and Jody. 'How did it go?' asked Jody. 'Did he see through your disguise?'

'No,' said Pete, climbing off Thomas's shoulders and removing the Lulubelle wig. 'And we nearly got to see the map.'

'Nearly?' said Jody. 'You mean you didn't see it?'

'I'm afraid not,' said Thomas.

'Did the old man refuse to show it to you?' Jody asked. 'Oh, and by the way, I knew I'd seen him somewhere before, and now I remember where. He's the old man who kept falling asleep in the governors' meeting. That's why he wouldn't let Mr Majeika into the library – he knows all about him.'

'He didn't refuse to show it to us,' said Pete. 'He went to the shelves and took out an old leather-bound folder with "MAP SHOWING WHERE TO FIND THE OLD BACK DOOR" on it in gold lettering. But when he opened the folder, it was empty.'

'He was very surprised and upset,' said Thomas. 'He said that an old lady and her grandson had visited the library earlier today, and had specially asked to see that map. But he couldn't believe they'd stolen it.'

'An old lady and her grandson?' repeated Mr Majeika. 'You don't think that they could really have been –'

'Wilhelmina Worlock and Hamish Bigmore,' said Pete. 'I'm dead certain they were, because in the folder where the map should have been was a tiny scrap of paper, and written on it was: "Tee hee! Got you this time, Majeika. W. W. and H. B."'

'I'm afraid there's no doubt about it, Mr Majeika,' said Thomas. 'Wilhelmina is going to make sure you don't get your magic powers back.'

'Yes,' said Mr Majeika gloomily. 'And another thought occurs to me,' he went on. 'If Wilhelmina and Hamish can find the Old Back Door, and get into the place where all the magic comes from, then

Hamish can get the magic powers that I've lost.'

'You mean …?' asked Jody.

Mr Majeika nodded. 'If we don't get there first,' he said, 'we won't be able to prevent Hamish from becoming a wizard!'

6. Cosy Corner

Just at that moment, Thomas spotted
Hamish Bigmore. He was walking past
the castle, carrying something big that
was wrapped up in brown paper. 'Look!'
whispered Thomas. 'There he is – and I
bet it's the map he's carrying.'

'Let's capture him,' said Pete, 'and
rescue the map.'

'No, not yet,' said Jody. 'First of all, we
should discover exactly what he's up to.
Don't you think so, Mr Majeika?'

Mr Majeika nodded. 'I'll tell you what,'

he said, 'I'll make us all invisible, and then it will be easy for us to follow Hamish without him spotting us.' He raised his hands as if he was going to do a spell – and then he remembered. 'Oh dear,' he said, 'I keep forgetting that I can't do magic any more.'

'Never mind, Mr Majeika,' said Jody, 'we can follow Hamish just as well without magic, if we do it carefully and make sure he doesn't see us. If we get too close to him, we can hide behind lamp posts and in shop doorways.'

They set off, doing just as Jody had suggested, and soon they had followed Hamish to the edge of the town, where there was a big supermarket with a car park. Thomas, Pete, Jody and Mr Majeika hid behind the cars, and they watched while Hamish amused himself by undoing a stack of supermarket trolleys, and pushing them hard so that they scattered around the car park.

'That's a stupid thing to do,' whispered Thomas. 'It's getting dark, and the cars will bump into the trolleys. Let's go and stop him.'

'No, don't,' whispered Jody. 'Look who's coming!'

A trolley had rolled into the car park without anyone pushing it. After a moment, Thomas realized what Jody meant, because sitting in the trolley and making it roll where she wanted by magic was Wilhelmina Worlock.

She made her trolley roll up silently behind Hamish and bump him on the bottom. He gave a yell and spun round, then saw that it was Wilhelmina.

'Don't you treat me like that!' he snapped. 'Do that again and I'll tear up your precious map into a million pieces.'

'Tee hee!' cackled Wilhelmina. 'Give me the map! I want it back in case that weaselly worm of a wizard Majeika gets his nasty little hands on it, and uses it to find his way to the Old Back Door so he can recover his magic powers. I'm not letting that happen, oh no!' And she tried to snatch the map from Hamish.

He dodged out of her way, and waved the parcel containing the map in the air. 'Why should I give it to you, you silly old bat?' he snapped at Wilhelmina. 'It's not yours – you stole it.'

'And so did *you*, my little Star Pupil,' said Wilhelmina. 'You helped me steal it and if you're not careful, I'll tell the police – ha ha!'

'Ouch!' cried Hamish, because Wilhelmina had waved her arms in the air and a fierce blue burst of what looked like electricity crackled from her hands across to his. He dropped the parcel and, before he could recover, Wilhelmina picked it up.

'Got it!' she snapped. 'I know you wanted to use it to find your own way to the Old Back Door, you slimy little toad, but you shan't! You shan't! Tee hee!' And, sniggering to herself, she made the supermarket trolley zoom up into the air. In a moment, she had vanished into the darkening sky.

'Stupid old bat,' muttered Hamish to himself. 'So she thinks she can stop me, just like that. The silly thing about witches and wizards is that they don't know about modern technology. She's obviously never heard of photocopying.' And from his pocket he took a big piece of folded paper.

'He's photocopied the map,' Jody whispered to Mr Majeika.

'Let's jump out at him, and snatch it from him,' whispered Thomas.

Pete shook his head. 'I don't think so,' he said. 'For all we know, Wilhelmina may be keeping a close eye on Hamish. They may be quarrelling right now, but if we pick a fight with him, she might just come to his rescue. Anyway, I've got

another idea. I reckon Hamish
photocopied it at a shop near his house – I
know the shop myself. Let's go there, just
in case.'

'Just in case what?' asked Jody.

'It's only a chance,' said Peter. 'You'll
see.'

So they left Hamish to go on with his
game of scattering the trolleys around the
car park, and hurried off in the direction
of his house.

'There it is!' said Pete after a few
minutes, pointing at a shop that said:
'COSY CORNER CANDY SHOP –
SWEETS, NEWSPAPERS &
PHOTOCOPYING'.

He led them into the shop – and then
gasped and stopped in his tracks, because
behind the counter was the old man with
the beard.

'Good evening, young fellow,' said the

old man. 'Can I help you?' He seemed to have lost his stammer.

'Do you work here in the evenings after the library has shut?' Pete asked him.

'Library?' said the old man. 'What library? I work here in this shop all day, young fellow.'

Jody was going to ask him if he was one of the school governors, but she decided to go straight to the point. 'Has there been a boy here today, doing some photocopying?' she asked.

The old man nodded. 'I think you could say so,' he answered. 'In a word, yes.'

'Please could we look through the rubbish bin,' asked Pete, 'to see if he threw away any copies because they didn't come out right?'

The old man nodded again. 'I think I could allow that,' he answered. He pointed to the waste-paper basket that stood beside the photocopier and watched while Pete searched through it. There were lots of bits of paper, but no sign of a copy of the map.

'It's no use,' said Pete finally to Thomas. 'You were right – we should have jumped on Hamish and taken it from him.'

'Are you perchance looking for *this*?'

asked the old man, holding up a crumpled sheet of paper. It had written on it: '*Map of Where to Find the Old Back Door – Top Secret*'. 'I saved this copy, which your young friend threw into the bin,' said the old man, 'because I thought that somebody else might be interested in it. There you are, my friends, and I hope you have fun with it.'

Pete took it from him, and said, 'Thank you very much. Are you *sure* you don't work at the library?'

'Perfectly sure,' said the old man. 'Oh, and before you go, don't forget *this*. It belongs with the map.' He handed them a small packet, labelled '*Not to be opened until you reach the First Place*'.

They thanked him again, walked out of the shop and took a close look at the map.

7. Off to the Wedding

'It isn't a map at all!' said Thomas. 'It's just an empty page with two words on it. That old man in the shop has cheated us. I'm going back to complain!' But when they turned round, they saw that the shop had shut, and when they looked through the window there was no sign of the old man.

'Well,' said Mr Majeika, 'I think it's a case of, never mind what we *haven't* got, let's take a closer look at what we *have* got.' He peered closely at the piece of paper and the two words written on it: 'Crown Jewels'.

Mr Majeika repeated them, '"Crown Jewels". Now,' he asked Jody, Thomas and Pete, 'what does that mean?'

'They're the jewels that belong to the Queen,' said Jody. 'I once went to see them.'

'Really?' said Mr Majeika. 'Does the Queen let people come to her house to have a look at them?'

'They're not in Buckingham Palace,' said Pete. 'They're in the Tower of London, and they're *very* heavily guarded.'

'Are we supposed to steal them?' asked Thomas.

Jody shook her head. 'I don't think so,' she said. 'But maybe when we get there, we'll find the Old Back Door.'

'Did you say this Tower was in

London?' asked Mr Majeika. 'We can get there by magic carpet. Oh – I forgot.' And he started to look very miserable.

'It's all right, Mr Majeika,' said Jody. 'We don't need a magic carpet to get there. We can catch a coach – but it's getting late and I think we shouldn't set off until tomorrow morning.'

Thomas and Pete wanted to go to London right away, and even Mr Majeika looked unhappy at the idea of waiting till the next day.

'It's all my fault,' he kept saying. 'If I hadn't been so stupid at Halloween, we wouldn't have had any of this trouble.'

Next morning, they were at the bus station bright and early, and quite soon the coach had dropped them in London, right outside the Tower.

'What a very grim-looking building,' said Mr Majeika. 'Perhaps they'll lock us

up in there if we do anything to the
Queen's jewels.'

'Look!' said Jody, pointing to a sign that
said: '*Please queue here for visits to the
Crown Jewels*'. 'Let's go and see them –
and keep our eyes open for anything
odd.'

'As long as it's not Wilhelmina
Worlock,' said Pete.

They joined the queue, and had to stand in it for nearly an hour, but finally they found themselves climbing some steps into a darkened chamber. In the middle of it were some big glass cases, heavily guarded by men in Beefeater uniforms.

The jewels were very beautiful, and there were several crowns, to be worn by the Queen at different times.

'Look!' said Jody, pointing at the most splendid of all the crowns. 'What's that folded up and lying in the middle of it?'

Pete gazed at it. 'It's a piece of paper, just like our so-called "map",' he said. He leant over the glass case as far as he could, in the hope of reading what was on it.

'Hoi, my lad, that's not allowed!' said one of the Beefeaters. 'Behave yourself, or you'll have to leave.'

'Oh dear,' sighed Mr Majeika. 'In the

old days I could have fetched it by magic. Wait a minute! Who's got that little packet we were given by the old man at the shop?'

'I have,' said Jody, taking it out of her pocket. 'It says, *"Not to be opened until you reach the First Place"*. Do you think this is the First Place?'

Mr Majeika nodded and took a close

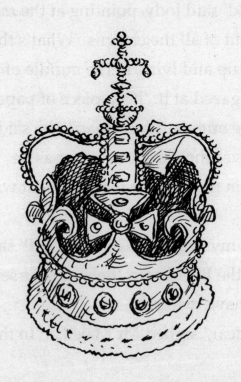

look at the little packet. He opened it up. 'There's some powder inside,' he said. 'I think I know what it is. It's magic, of course, so I shouldn't be using it – but *you* can!' And he handed the packet back to Jody, and whispered some instructions in her ear.

Jody nodded. 'I'll do my best,' she whispered back at him. 'Tell me when to do it. Wouldn't it be best to wait until everyone else has gone?' she said, looking around at all the other visitors who had come to see the Crown Jewels.

'It'll probably work,' muttered Mr Majeika. 'Do it now!'

Jody scattered a handful of the magic powder in the air. All at once, everyone froze. Nothing moved, and all the tourists looking at the Crown Jewels, and the Beefeaters, seemed to have been turned to stone.

Amazingly, the glass case containing the crown unlocked itself and swung open. Silently, the piece of paper floated up from the crown, out of the glass case and into Jody's hand.

A few seconds later, everyone unfroze again. The Beefeaters didn't seem to notice that anything odd had happened, and the glass case had locked itself up again. Jody unfolded the new piece of paper. Like the first one, it had just two words on it: 'BBC news'.

'It's a sort of treasure hunt, isn't it, Mr Majeika?' asked Pete, when he had seen what was written on the paper. 'You go to the place it tells you, and when you get there, you pick up the next clue.'

'That's right,' said Mr Majeika. 'But I don't know what it means by "BBC news".'

'It's simple, Mr Majeika,' said Jody.

'We've got to go to the place where they broadcast the BBC television news. I went there once, to be in the audience for a programme, and I know where it is. Come on!'

Just an hour later, they had managed to join a tour of the BBC television studios.

'The next thing we're going to see,' said the guide, 'is a live broadcast of the lunchtime news. In we all go – but no one is to make a sound!'

'Look, Mr Majeika!' murmured Thomas as they tiptoed into the news studio. 'I can see our next piece of paper. It's stuck to the newsreader's desk. Get ready with the "freeze" powder, Jody.'

A red light flashed, and the newsreader picked up her script and started to smile at the camera. Jody threw a handful of the powder in the air, and once again everyone froze. The piece of paper unstuck itself from the desk and floated into Jody's hand. This time the words on it were 'Cup Final'.

'This is going to be a difficult one!' said Thomas, when they had all unfrozen and come out of the news studio. 'Do you know what the Cup Final is, Mr Majeika?'

Mr Majeika shook his head.

'It's the most important of all the football matches,' Pete explained, 'and they're playing it this afternoon. If we hurry, we can get there in time – but we haven't got tickets, so they won't let us in.'

But in the end, the freeze powder did the trick. Jody threw a little more of it in the air as soon as they arrived at the football stadium, and while everyone froze the piece of paper came flying over the stadium roof and into Jody's hand.

'I expect it was stuck to the ball,' said Jody.

The words on it this time were: 'Royal wedding'.

'This is going to be *really* difficult,' said Jody. 'Do you know about the Royal wedding that's happening today in Westminster Abbey?'

They all nodded.

'Well,' said Jody, 'we're supposed to go to it to look for our next clue! And there's only a tiny bit of the freeze powder left. I'm sure it won't work.'

8. The Old Back Door

But the Royal wedding turned out to be
as easy as the Crown Jewels, the BBC
news and the Cup Final. They waited in
the crowd until the royal couple came out
of Westminster Abbey, and sure enough
Jody spotted the piece of paper attached
to the bride's veil. While everyone was
cheering, she threw the last of the freeze
powder in the air, and everyone froze
immediately – even the bells that were
pealing loudly – until the piece of paper
had floated over to Jody.

'I don't believe it,' she said, looking at the two words on it. 'It just says "Class Three". What's that supposed to mean?'

'I think,' said Mr Majeika, 'it means we should go back to school.'

So they did. By the time the coach had brought them home from London, school had ended for the day, so there was no one around to watch Mr Majeika tiptoeing into his old classroom with Jody, Thomas and Pete. The room was empty.

'So what do we do now?' asked Thomas.

At that moment, the door of the big cupboard creaked open, and a voice said, 'Welcome to the Old Back Door.'

It was the old man – the one who had been the school governor, the person in charge of the Oldest Library in the World, and the shopkeeper. Seeing him again, Mr Majeika scratched his head.

'Now why didn't I recognize you before?' he said. Then he turned to Jody, Thomas and Pete. 'This is a very important person,' he told them. 'The Chief Wizard.'

The Chief Wizard bowed to them. 'I've been trying to sort things out since our friend Majeika got himself into trouble, but the rules said that I couldn't make it too easy for him. Yes, this is the Old Back Door, which leads from the ordinary

world into the world of magic.'

'And it's in our very own school, and our very own classroom?' asked Jody.

'Yes,' said the Chief Wizard. 'That's how we wizards knew about St Barty's School and Class Three. We used to peep at you all sometimes through the keyhole. We could see how nice you all were – well, almost all of you – and that's how we decided that you deserved to have a wizard as a teacher.'

'Thank you very much,' said Thomas. 'And now, please can Mr Majeika have his magic powers back?'

The Chief Wizard frowned. 'I'm afraid I've got some bad news,' he said gloomily. 'I knew it might happen as soon as Hamish Bigmore stole the map from the Oldest Library in the World.'

'So you didn't mean to let him steal it?' asked Jody.

The Chief Wizard shook his head. 'Certainly not,' he said. 'I failed to recognize him. We knew that you had a troublemaker in the class, but when he came to the library I didn't realize who he was.'

'So what's the bad news?' asked Jody anxiously.

'Well,' answered the Chief Wizard, 'the rules say that anyone who finds the Old Back Door gets his or her magic powers back, if they've been lost. And if they haven't ever had magic powers, they can get them and become a wizard or a witch. You see, Majeika's magic powers have been waiting here for him to reclaim them. But I'm afraid they have to go to the first person who turns up and asks for them. And I'm very sorry to say that someone else did get here first, before all of you, and he's laid claim to Majeika's magic. Step forward Learner-Wizard Bigmore!'

Jody, Thomas and Pete groaned as, out of the cupboard, there stepped Hamish in a wizard's cloak and hat, with a wand in one hand and a spell book tucked under his other arm.

'Ha ha ha!' he said, in his nastiest voice.

'Now I can *really* get my revenge on you, Mr Majeika.' And he raised his magic wand in the air.

'Wait a minute, Learner-Wizard Bigmore,' said the Chief Wizard. 'First of all, every new wizard has to take a Magic Test, before he can be granted a full wizard's licence.'

Hamish scowled. 'You didn't tell me that,' he grumbled. 'I demand fair treatment!'

Suddenly there was a whooshing noise, and Wilhelmina Worlock flew past the window on her shopping trolley. She landed it in the playground, and hurried into Class Three.

'Is my Star Pupil going to do his Magic Test?' she cackled. 'Take my advice, young Hamish, and look up all the spells in your book before you try them out.'

'Who cares about that stupid old book?'

said Hamish. 'I know how to do all the spells – I've learnt them by watching Mr Majeika, and they're easy-peasy. Any old fool can do them.'

'If it's as easy as you say, Hamish,' remarked the Chief Wizard, 'we won't waste any more time. Let's start right away, with the first question. Learner-Wizard Bigmore, make yourself invisible, so that no one can see you.'

Hamish shut his eyes and muttered some words. They must have been the wrong ones, because he didn't become invisible at all. He turned bright green, and smoke came out of his nose and ears.

'Nought out of ten,' said the Chief Wizard. 'Second question. Learner-Wizard Bigmore, make yourself rise in the air and float above the ground.'

'That's easy-peasy,' said Hamish, and he closed his eyes and muttered a spell

again. This time he almost got it right, because Thomas, Pete, Jody, Mr Majeika, the Chief Wizard and Wilhelmina Worlock all rose up in the air. But Hamish himself stayed firmly on the ground.

'Minus five,' said the Chief Wizard. 'You get a penalty for doing the right spell to the wrong people. Now, this is your last chance, Learner-Wizard Bigmore. For your third and final question, make somebody else look like you. I need a volunteer for this one – Wilhelmina Worlock, you'll do fine.'

Wilhelmina grumbled like mad, but in the end she stepped forward and stood opposite Hamish. He closed his eyes and muttered a spell – and nothing happened to Wilhelmina. Hamish, however, changed completely – into a smaller version of Miss Worlock, except that on his head was the 'Lulubelle' blonde wig.

'Nought out of ten,' said the Chief Wizard. 'Learner-Wizard Bigmore is herewith deprived of his magic powers. They revert to Mr Majeika, who becomes a full wizard again.'

'Do you mean he gets his spell book back, and he can do magic once more?' asked Pete, as Thomas and Jody cheered at the good news.

'That's right,' answered the Chief
Wizard. 'Remember, Majeika, you're not
supposed to do magic at all, now that
you're a teacher. But I shan't be watching
that closely!' And he gave a wink.

'You stupid idiot!' Wilhelmina Worlock
screamed at Hamish Bigmore. 'I'll never
call you my Star Pupil again, you
brainless little weasel.'

Hamish was tugging at the wig, but it wouldn't come off his head, and he still looked exactly like Miss Worlock. 'I think we'll let him stay like that for a bit, shall we?' said the Chief Wizard. 'Maybe until next Halloween?'